Daniel Learns to Ride a Bike

Adapted by Becky Friedman

Based on the screenplay "Daniel's Bicycle" written by Leah Gotcsik

Poses and layouts by Jason Fruchter

Simon Spotlight

New York   London   Toronto   Sydney   New Delhi

SIMON SPOTLIGHT

An imprint of Simon & Schuster Children's Publishing Division
1230 Avenue of the Americas, New York, New York 10020
This Simon Spotlight paperback edition December 2018
© 2018 The Fred Rogers Company
All rights reserved, including the right of reproduction in whole or in part in any form.
SIMON SPOTLIGHT and colophon are registered trademarks of Simon & Schuster, Inc.
For information about special discounts for bulk purchases, please contact Simon & Schuster
Special Sales at 1-866-506-1949 or business@simonandschuster.com.
Manufactured in the United States of America 1118 LAK
10 9 8 7 6 5 4 3 2 1
ISBN 978-1-5344-3086-0
ISBN 978-1-5344-3087-7 (eBook)

It was a beautiful day in the Neighborhood of Make-Believe, and Daniel Tiger was helping Mom Tiger in the garden. Suddenly Daniel heard a sound. It sounded like ringing!

"Mom, do you hear that sound?" asked Daniel.

"I do hear it," said Mom. "I wonder where it's coming from."

Daniel looked around to see where the sound was coming from.
"Hello! *Ring! Ring!* Where are you?" called Daniel.
Daniel walked through his yard, past his playhouse, until he found . . .

Dad Tiger standing next to a shiny red bike, ringing the bell. *Ring! Ring!*

"Dad!" said Daniel. "Why do you have a bike?"

"This was my bike when I was a little tiger," Dad told Daniel. "But now I'm giving it to you!"

Daniel gave Dad a big hug. "Thank you, Dad. Can I ride it now?"

"You sure can," said Dad. "Let's put your helmet on first, and then we can go."

"Yay!" said Daniel happily.

Dad helped Daniel get on the bike, and he started to pedal. "Here I go! *Vroom! Vroom!*" said Daniel, giggling.

Daniel wiggled and wobbled. He wobbled and he wiggled. "Riding this bike is hard!" he said.

Daniel started to pedal again, slowly.

♪ *"Grr-grr-grr out loud. Keep on trying and you'll feel proud!"* ♪ ♪ Daniel sang.

Daniel wiggled and he wobbled. He wobbled and he wiggled. And then slowly . . . he started to move forward!

"I'm doing it!" shouted Daniel proudly. "I'm riding my bike!"

"Dad, can I ride my bike all the way to the park?" asked Daniel.

"Okay," said Dad. "Let's go!"

Daniel rode his bike until he came to the bottom of a big hill.

"Uh-oh," said Daniel. "How do I go up this big hill?"

"Hold on to the handlebars and push hard on the pedals," said Dad.

Daniel held on to the handlebars,
and he pushed hard on the pedals.
He pushed harder . . .

and harder . . .

but he still couldn't make it up to
the top of the hill!
   "It's too hard," said Daniel.
"I can't do it."

Daniel kept on trying. *"Grr-grr-grr,"* he said out loud. Then he pushed and he pedaled up, and up, and up until finally . . .

"I made it to the top of the hill!" said Daniel.

"How do you feel?" asked Dad.

"Proud," said Daniel with a big smile. "And look, there's the park!" He giggled as he continued to pedal.

At the park Daniel saw his friends Prince Wednesday and Chrissie. Prince Wednesday's brother, Prince Tuesday, was there too!

"Royally great bike!" said Prince Wednesday.

"It looks really fast," said Chrissie.

"Thanks," said Daniel. "I like the bell. *Ring! Ring!*"

Daniel, Chrissie, and Prince Wednesday decided to play on the rings.
"I want to swing all the way across," said Prince Wednesday.
"You can do it!" cheered Chrissie.
But when Prince Wednesday tried, he couldn't make it across the rings.
Prince Wednesday was upset.
"This is hard," he said sadly.

"You can do it, Prince Wednesday," said Daniel. *"Grr-grr-grr out loud. Keep on trying and you'll feel proud!"* "Okay, I'll keep trying," said Prince Wednesday.

Prince Wednesday reached for the first ring, and then the second ring, and then the third ring.

"Grr-grr-grr out loud. Keep on trying and you'll feel proud!" Prince Wednesday sang as he reached for each ring. At last Prince Wednesday made it all the way across the rings!

"I did it!" shouted Prince Wednesday. "I feel so proud."

Swinging on the rings looked like so much fun, Daniel imagined that he had to swing on rings to get everywhere!

Daniel, Chrissie, and Prince Wednesday took turns swinging and hanging on the rings.

Chrissie could hang on the rings for eight whole seconds without letting go!

"Chrissie is really strong," said Prince Wednesday.

At last it was time for Daniel to go home.
"Can I ride my bike home?" Daniel asked Dad.
"You bet," said Dad.

"Riding a bike is hard to do!" said Daniel. "But I *grr*-ed and *grr*-ed and kept trying. And I'm proud that I did it. What are you trying to learn? Ugga Mugga!"

Do you want to learn more
about bikes and bike safety
with the help of a parent, guardian,
or caregiver? Read on for
some helpful advice
from Daniel Tiger!

There are lots of different types of bikes. Some are just right for riding in town, and some are better for riding on rougher paths. There are even bikes that fold up so they are easier to carry!

What are bikes used for?

- Some people use bikes to go to school or work.
- Messengers use bikes to deliver mail or other packages quickly.
- Police officers often use bikes to get around in both small towns and big cities.

Many people ride bikes for fun. Do you ride a bike or a tricycle? Where do you like to ride?

Dear Parents and Caregivers,

Is your child ready to learn to ride a bike? Here are some tips to help them choose one:

- Remember to choose a bike that's the right size for their height.
- Your child should be able to stand over the top tube of their bike. Both of their feet should be flat on the ground.
- If they haven't tried riding a bike before, they can always ride a tricycle first.

Tip from Daniel Tiger:
"I always wear a helmet
when I ride a bike or a
tricycle."

Where to Ride Your Bike

Daniel Tiger learned to ride his bike in the Neighborhood of Make-Believe. It's important to learn to ride somewhere safe and away from traffic. Always make sure an adult is present when your child is riding. Some places to keep in mind are the park, your driveway, or the playground. Don't forget to keep an eye out for cars and other people!

Important Bike Safety

- Always wear a bike helmet and have your child wear one too. Even if it's a short ride, your heads should always be protected!
- Always have your child wear brightly colored clothing so cars and people can see them. Make sure shoelaces are tied and tucked into shoes, and avoid loose pant legs.
- Your child should always stay close to a trusted adult.

"It's fun trying something new, but sometimes it can be hard. Just remember to keep trying, and you will feel proud of what you can do!"